The Mystery of the Magi's Treasure

THREE COUSINS DETECTIVE CLUB®

YOUNG COUSINS MYSTERIES

The Mystery of the Magi's Treasure

Elspeth Campbell Murphy

Illustrated by Joe Nordstrom

BETHANY HOUSE PUBLISHERS

MINNEAPOLIS, MINNESOTA 55438

The Mystery of the Magi's Treasure
Copyright © 1995
Elspeth Campbell Murphy

Cover and story illustrations by Joe Nordstrom

Three Cousins Detective Club® and TCDC® are registered
trademarks of Elspeth Campbell Murphy

Published by Bethany House Publishers
A Ministry of Bethany Fellowship International
11400 Hampshire Avenue South
Minneapolis, Minnesota 55438
www.bethanyhouse.com

Printed in the United States of America by
Bethany Press International, Minneapolis, Minnesota 55438

Library of Congress Cataloging-in-Publication Data

Murphy, Elspeth Campbell.
    The mystery of the Magi's treasure / Elspeth Campbell Murphy ;
[illustrated by Joe Nordstrom].
        p. cm. — (Three Cousins Detective Club® ; bk. 6)
    Summary: While celebrating "Christmas in July," the three cousins
come into some stolen art works and discover that even bad boys can be
good.

    [1. Mystery and detective stories. 2. Cousins—Fiction.
3. Conduct of life—Fiction.] I. Nordstrom, Joe, ill. II. Title.
III. Series: Murphy, Elspeth Campbell. Three Cousins Detective Club®
; 6.
PZ7.M95316Mydd   1995
[Fic]—dc20   95–7097
ISBN 1–55661–410–1   CIP
                                            AC

In loving memory of my father-in-law,
Howard R. Murphy,
whose life was filled with
love, joy, peace,
patience, kindness, goodness,
faithfulness, gentleness, and self-control.

ELSPETH CAMPBELL MURPHY has been a familiar name in Christian publishing for over fifteen years, with more than seventy-five books to her credit and sales reaching five million worldwide. She is the author of the best-selling series *David and I Talk to God* and *The Kids From Apple Street Church*, as well as the 1990 Gold Medallion winner *Do You See Me, God?* A graduate of Trinity College and Moody Bible Institute, Elspeth and her husband, Mike, make their home in Chicago, where she writes full time.

Contents

1

The Kevins

*T*imothy Dawson sometimes wondered what it would be like to be really, really bad.

Not the kind of bad where you beat up on people or steal things. But just the kind of bad where you were always acting up and goofing off and no one ever expected you to behave yourself.

Timothy sometimes wondered what it would be like to be one of the Kevins.

The Kevins were three boys who went to the church where Timothy's grandfather was the pastor. Timothy and his cousins Sarah-Jane Cooper and Titus McKay knew the Kevins slightly from being in the same Sunday school class with them when the cousins visited. But it was more like they knew *of* the Kevins.

But then—everybody knew *of* the Kevins. The three boys had met when they had all toddled into the same nursery Sunday school class on the same day. They had been together ever since. Every teacher they'd ever known had declared, "Those three boys should be separated!"

But somehow Kevin O'Connell, Kevin Jones, and Kevin Weston had managed to stay together. Always acting up and goofing off. And no one ever expected them to behave themselves.

And that's how—on the hottest day of the summer so far—Timothy, Titus, and Sarah-Jane came to be wearing long, flowing robes and fancy crowns.

They were supposed to be the Three Wise Men.

They were not too happy about it.

And it was all because of the Kevins.

2

Christmas in July

*I*t had happened like this:

The resort town where the cousins' grandparents lived got a lot of tourists in the summertime. And there were a lot of artists who lived there all year round.

So every summer the town sponsored a sidewalk art fair. This year the theme was "Christmas in July," and everyone was going all out.

Even the churches had gotten involved. They had joined together for a free outdoor concert and carol sing-along, complete with peppermint ice cream and Christmas cookies.

The problem was making sure that visitors knew about the concert. The churches had put up posters, of course.

But then someone thought it would be a good idea to have church people go among the crowds to hand out leaflets.

And then someone else said that this sounded like a good job for the kids.

And then someone else said it would be cute to have the kids dressed as angels and shepherds.

And then someone else said not to forget the Three Wise Men.

So it was decided that a few kids from each church would go around in costumes handing out leaflets about the concert. All the other kids would be in the choir.

The trouble came when someone, who didn't know of the Kevins, picked *them* to be the Three Wise Men.

When Timothy heard about this, he couldn't wait to see what would happen. At Christmastime, whichever kids played the Wise Men walked in single file slowly and solemnly down the center aisle as the choir sang, "We Three Kings of Orient Are."

It would be a change to see the Three Kings knocking one another's crowns off and rolling around in the dirt.

And that's exactly what happened at rehearsal.

"No, no, no, no, no!" said the choir director, who *did* know of the Kevins. "This will never do. We need three completely dependable children to be the Wise Men."

The cousins should have seen what was coming. But they didn't.

As the Kevins scrambled out of their costumes, the choir director scanned the choir for

replacements. He found them.

"Timothy! Titus! Sarah-Jane! Get down here. On the double."

The Kevins were put in the choir—as far apart as the director could get them without knocking people off the risers.

The cousins slumped into the Wise Men costumes and picked up their leaflets.

The robes were hot.

The crowns were heavy.

Timothy caught sight of the Kevins. They were grinning.

He doubted the Kevins were anywhere near as dumb as they pretended to be.

3

Bragging Grandma

The choir director came over to check on the cousins. "There now," he said heartily. "You know what to do? Good. Then we're all set. I know you'll do a great job. Your grandmother is always telling us how intelligent and responsible and polite you three are."

It's a good thing for him we're so polite, thought Timothy. *Too polite to say what we think of being pulled out of the choir to dress up as the Wise Men in the middle of July. Those lucky kids in the choir don't even have to wear their robes until dress rehearsal.*

The director went back to the choir, and the cousins were left to themselves.

"Well, you guys," said Sarah-Jane. "Looks like Grandma strikes again."

The boys knew right away what she meant. It was a standing joke in the family how much Grandma BRAGGED about her grandchildren.

"It's our own fault, really," said Titus with a dramatic sigh. "If only we weren't such *wonderful* children!"

Timothy laughed. But he saw the serious side of it, too. The problem with everybody thinking you were a good kid was that you couldn't exactly complain about it. It wasn't as if people were calling you names or anything. . . .

Just then some tourists passed by. He heard one of them say, "Oh, look, honey! The Three Magi! Aren't they just *adorable*?"

"That does it," Timothy muttered to his cousins. "We have *got* to tell Grandma to stop bragging about us. Look where it's gotten us. Let's ask her to make them get some other kids to be the Wise Men."

Titus and Sarah-Jane nodded. But they didn't have time to say anything.

It just so happened Grandma was coming by at the same time. And she had overheard

16

what the lady had said about the adorable Wise
Men.

"They're my grandchildren, you know,"
she announced to this complete stranger.

"Oh, are they *really*?" cried the lady. "You
must be very proud."

"Oh, I am!" said Grandma. "They're just
as good as gold. The three of them are visiting
their grandpa and me. And they never give us
a minute's trouble."

The cousins glanced at one another. How
could they make a stink about being the adorable Magi now?

After chatting for a while, the people
moved on, and Grandma turned back to the
cousins.

"I'm glad I ran into you," she said. "I was
just coming to tell you I'm going out for a
while. Grandpa's in his study with Gubbio if
you need anything."

Gubbio was Titus's little dog. For once the
cousins were glad he wasn't trotting along at
their heels. It was bad enough being the Three
Wise Men without being the Three Wise Men
and a Yorkshire terrier.

"Where are you going?" Sarah-Jane asked Grandma.

"Did I ever mention my young friend Sylvia?"

"The artist?" asked Timothy.

"That's right," said Grandma. "She's what you might call a 'folk artist.' She hasn't been to art school. And I think she feels inferior to some of the artists around here. Anyway, I heard that one of the gallery owners, Mr. Fitzgerald, is very open to showing new folk art. I want to encourage Sylvia to take a few pieces to show him."

Grandma hurried off, and Timothy wished that he could go with her.

This past year at school, art had become his all-time favorite subject. And he loved putzing around at home, just making stuff. He wondered what sort of art Sylvia made.

But for now, he had a job to do.

4

Something Odd

The job of handing out leaflets wasn't nearly as bad as Timothy had thought it was going to be. People were delighted to hear about the concert. And everyone was very nice.

Sure, it was annoying the way people kept telling them how cute they looked in their costumes. But the cousins made themselves get over it.

So everything was going fine.

Until something odd happened.

A frazzled-looking lady came rushing up to them.

"There you are!" she cried. "I've been looking all over for you!"

The cousins blinked. As far as they knew,

they had never met this person before in their lives.

"Us?" asked Timothy. "You were looking for us?"

"You're the Three Wise Men, aren't you?" replied the lady.

The cousins glanced at one another. In these getups, who else would they be?

But before they could answer, the lady thrust three boxes into their hands.

"Here. The Wise Men are supposed to have gifts for Baby Jesus, aren't they? Your costumes aren't complete without them. So here's the gold. And that incense stuff. And the um—"

20

"Myrrh?" said Titus.

"Right, right. The . . . myrrh. OK. Now, you hold on to those boxes, you hear me?"

"Whatever you do, don't lose them. And don't give them to anyone else but me. I'm the one in charge of the um—"

"Props?" said Titus.

"Right, right. The . . . props."

The woman turned to leave.

"Wait a minute," said Sarah-Jane, looking anxiously at the throngs of people. "How will we find you when we're done handing out leaflets?"

"Don't worry about that," said the lady briskly. "I'll find you. In those costumes, it will be easy to find you in the crowd."

"Wait a minute," said Timothy. He could hear his voice getting whiny. But the grown-ups kept making this job harder and harder. "How are we supposed to hold on to these boxes and hand out leaflets at the same time?"

Apparently the lady didn't want to hear any complaints, because she hurried away without answering.

5

Gold, Frankincense, and Myrrh

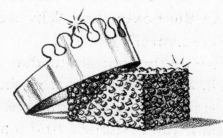

"*T*his is a nuisance," said Sarah-Jane, trying to hold on to her box with one hand and her leaflets with the other.

Titus agreed. "I don't see why we need to carry the presents at all. Why can't we just be the Wise Men *after* they found Jesus? They wouldn't have the presents with them then."

Sarah-Jane and Timothy had to agree that this made perfect sense. But what could they do?

Titus paused for a moment. Then he said, "You know what's funny?"

"Funny ha-ha? Or funny weird?" asked Sarah-Jane.

"Funny weird," said Titus.

"What is?" asked Sarah-Jane.

"OK," said Titus. "We already agreed that it's funny weird that we have to pass out leaflets *and* carry boxes at the same time. But why are we getting the boxes *now*? Why weren't they with the costumes?"

Sarah-Jane thought about that for a minute. "Well, all the churches are going together on this, right? So maybe someone from one church made the costumes. And maybe someone from another church made the props."

"Makes sense," said Titus. "And the prop lady was just running late. That's why she didn't give us the boxes till now. Right?"

"Right . . ." said Sarah-Jane. But she didn't sound as if she were buying her own explanation.

"So what's bothering you about it?" asked Titus.

The three cousins often talked things through like this. They had a detective club, and they always perked up when they came upon something odd.

Sometimes something that seemed odd at

first turned out later to have a logical explanation.

But sometimes something just seemed out of whack, and you couldn't explain it away.

The cousins had solved a lot of mysteries, and they had developed a kind of sense about these things. A feeling that something is wrong. But you don't know what. Or what it means.

That's what it felt like now.

The cousins had also discovered that talking about the mystery could help to solve it.

"OK," said Sarah-Jane slowly, thinking out loud. "This lady is in charge of the Christmas-story props. Right? But she doesn't even know the names of the Wise Men's gifts. The only one she got right was gold. I mean, doesn't that strike you as odd?"

"Yes, now that you mention it," said Titus. "Gold. Frankincense. And myrrh. I didn't know what frankincense and myrrh were until my Sunday school teacher told us. They're like rare, expensive perfume that you would bring to honor someone very important.

"But even before I knew what the words *meant*, I knew what the words *were*. This lady didn't even know what the words were. And she's the one in charge of the boxes."

"Speaking of the boxes . . ." said Timothy. He had been following his cousins' conversation and thinking his own thoughts all at the same time. "There's something wrong with them, too."

Titus and Sarah-Jane took a good look at their boxes for the first time. Then they looked at Timothy in surprise.

"What's wrong with them, Tim?" asked Titus. "They're EXcellent!"

"Absolutely beautiful!" agreed Sarah-Jane.

"My point exactly," said Timothy.

6

Beautiful Boxes

As detectives, the cousins had trained themselves to notice things. But Timothy was an artist as well as a detective. And that was why he noticed something odd about the boxes: They were *too* beautiful.

Timothy had once made a jewelry box as a present for his mother. First, he had emptied his rock collection out of his best cigar box. Then he had taken a bunch of macaroni in all kinds of different shapes and glued them close together, all over the lid. Finally, he had asked his father to help him spray-paint the whole box gold.

His mother had said it was the most beautiful box she had ever seen. She had even lent the box to the church for the Christmas pageant.

But Timothy knew his beautiful box was nowhere near as beautiful as these.

"Think about it," he said to his cousins. "When have you ever seen Christmas pageant props that look this good? What do the Wise Men carry at your church?"

Titus and Sarah-Jane closed their eyes, trying to picture it.

"An empty bubble-bath jar sprinkled with glitter," said Titus.

"Something like that," said Sarah-Jane.

"Same here," said Timothy. "But now look at these boxes."

The cousins looked at them again. The boxes had started out as plain old wooden boxes, probably. But someone had painted them with gorgeous colors—so shiny and luscious you just wanted to lick them. And then, on top of that, little objects had been glued in beautiful patterns.

When you looked very closely, you could see that the objects were common, everyday things. Colored glass. Buttons. Keys. Bottle caps. Even little plastic gumball machine toys.

Junk. The kind of things people throw away. But on these boxes the junk was all part of a master design.

Where most people saw junk, the person who made these boxes saw good stuff to work with.

It was then that Titus and Sarah-Jane realized what Timothy had noticed first.

They were looking at good, good work. Whoever had made these boxes was a real artist.

"But why are they using such special boxes as props?" asked Sarah-Jane.

Timothy shrugged. "I have no idea."

"Whatever the reason," said Titus, "the prop lady isn't taking any chance on something happening to them. She's over there behind you. Watching us."

7

Missing

Sarah-Jane and Timothy knew better than to whirl around yelling, "Where? Where?" when Titus said they were being watched.

Rather, they just looked around very, very casually. And when they spotted the prop lady, they gave no sign at all that they had noticed her.

They just turned back casually to face Titus.

"Why is she watching us?" muttered Sarah-Jane. "To make sure we don't lose the boxes? If she's that worried, why did she give them to us in the first place? Or why doesn't she just come get them back?"

Without knowing exactly why, the cousins held on to the boxes a little tighter.

Then—when Titus said, "It's all right; she's going away now"—all three of them gave a little sigh of relief.

"What's wrong with us?" asked Timothy. "What are we so jumpy about?"

None of them had an answer for that.

But at least they figured out what to do with their leaflets.

They went up to the booth of an artist they knew and set their beautiful boxes on the ground. It felt good to give their hands a rest. But they still guarded the boxes with their feet.

The artist let them put the leaflets on a corner of his table. They didn't have all that many left. So they put them in a pile. They weighted the leaflets down with a rock so they wouldn't blow away.

Then they borrowed a marking pen and some masking tape. On the back of one leaflet they printed in big letters: FREE! PLEASE TAKE ONE! HELP YOURSELF! They taped the sign to the awning pole right beside the pile of leaflets. This way, the leaflets could sort of pass themselves out.

The cousins were just wondering what to do next when another artist hurried up to the

booth with a warning for his friend.

"Keep an eye on your stuff," he said. "Some art pieces are missing, and no one has any idea where they could be."

8

The T.C.D.C.

"What happened?" asked Timothy, instantly tuning in to a mystery.

"Well, it was the strangest thing," said the artist's friend, whose name tag said *Bob*. "I heard that some artist—I didn't recognize the name—had stopped in at a gallery to show some of her pieces to the owner.

"The person who told me about it didn't know what the work looked like. I got the impression it was something offbeat and unusual.

"Anyway, the gallery hadn't opened for the day, yet. But the artist met a woman just outside the front door of the gallery. The woman said she was the owner's assistant."

"But was she really?" asked Titus.

Both artists looked at the cousins in surprise.

"You kids are pretty quick, aren't you?" said the artist they knew, whose name was John.

The cousins gave embarrassed little shrugs. What could you say to that? Well, yes, we are?

Sarah-Jane said, "It's just that we're the members of the T.C.D.C. So we're interested in these things."

"What's a 'teesy-deesy'?" asked John.

"It's letters," explained Timothy. "Capital T. Capital C. Capital D. Capital C. It stands for the Three Cousins Detective Club."

"Oh," said Bob. "Then this will be right up your alley."

He went on with the story. "It turns out this woman was *not* the gallery assistant. But the artist didn't know that at the time. And she had no reason to be suspicious. The 'assistant' was very friendly and helpful. She told the artist that the gallery owner was away—but that she would see that he got the artwork. She even wrote the artist a receipt."

"Then what happened?" asked Sarah-Jane.

"How did the artist find out something was wrong?"

"Good question," said Bob. "A little bit later, the artist thought of something she wanted to ask. So she went back to the gallery. It was open by then. The owner, Mr. Fitzgerald, was there. But his assistant—his *real* assistant—was on a trip. A thousand miles away! The so-called assistant was nowhere to be seen. And neither was the artwork. I wish I could remember the artist's name. I'm not familiar with her work at all."

The cousins looked at one another. They had a sinking feeling that they were all guessing the same thing.

Timothy said, "Her name wouldn't be Sylvia, would it?"

9

Sylvia

"*T*hat's it!" cried Bob. "Sylvia! That was the name. Sylvia. But how in the world did you kids know that?"

"Well, we're not positive," said Timothy. "But our grandmother has an artist friend named Sylvia who does really good work. Only Sylvia's really shy about it. So our grandmother told her to show some of her work to Mr. Fitzgerald."

John said, "What kind of stuff does Sylvia do? Painting? Pottery?"

Timothy shrugged. "We haven't actually seen it ourselves. Grandma just called it 'folk art.' That's why she told Sylvia to talk to Mr. Fitzgerald. She heard he likes that kind of thing."

Bob and John nodded. Bob said, "Sounds like your grandmother gave Sylvia some good advice."

"Yes," said Titus. "But it sure didn't work out very well! Poor Grandma. I know it's not her fault. But, knowing Grandma, she'll feel terrible about it."

"And poor Sylvia!" said Sarah-Jane. "The stuff must be long gone by now."

"Not necessarily," said Bob. "That's what I meant when I said that no one knows where the art could be."

The cousins looked at him eagerly.

He explained. "Well, it's possible, of course, that the thief got clean away—and, as Sarah-Jane said, the artwork is long gone.

"But getting away would be tricky. It's hard to move in these crowds. And how could the thief be sure Sylvia wouldn't see her walking off with the artwork? It would be safer to hide it and just lay low for a while. So it's just possible the thief stashed the pieces somewhere. And that she's planning to come back for them later."

The cousins and John agreed with Bob that it was just possible the art was still hidden somewhere.

But where?

Bob went on. "The problem is, hiding the stuff would be tricky, too. Where could the thief hide the art without anyone seeing her do it? And how could she hide it where no one else could get it? It would have to be a place where no one would think to look. Where would you find such a good hiding place in such a hurry?"

"Beats me," said John. "This sounds like a job for the T.C.D.C."

"I'm afraid it beats the T.C.D.C., too," said Sarah-Jane with a sigh.

There was nothing more to say.

Bob had to get back to his own booth.

John had to wait on a customer.

And the cousins had to walk around looking wise.

They picked up their boxes and wandered off.

They hadn't gone all that far before they stopped dead in their tracks.

They knew what Sylvia's artwork looked like.

They knew who had taken it.

And they knew exactly where it was hidden.

10

The Perfect Hiding Place

"*I* saw this movie once," said Timothy to his cousins as they set off through the crowds for their grandparents' house.

"In the movie, everybody was going crazy trying to find this really big diamond. An old man had hidden it in his house. Only he died before he could tell anybody where it was. The relatives tore the place up looking for a secret hiding place. But the diamond was right out in the open the whole time. People passed it a dozen times a day. But they didn't even see it."

"Where was it?" cried Sarah-Jane and Titus, dying of curiosity.

Timothy paused, making the most of the moment. "In the crystal chandelier," he said.

"Aha!" cried Sarah-Jane. "That was the

perfect hiding place—because the diamond blended right in with the cut glass!"

"EXcellent!" agreed Titus. "What do they call it when that happens?"

Timothy and Sarah-Jane waited to see if Titus would come up with the answer to his own question. He often did that. It was his way of thinking out loud.

"Got it!" said Titus. "'Hidden in plain sight.' That's what they call it when something is right out in the open. But people don't see it, because it's—what's that word? Camouflaged."

"And it's like Grandpa says," added Sarah-Jane. "People see what they expect to see. And they don't see what they don't expect to see."

Timothy and Titus knew exactly what Sarah-Jane was talking about.

Of course, no one would expect to see stolen art being carried around out in the open by three kids.

But what if it were Christmas in July?

And what if those three kids were dressed as the Magi in long, flowing robes and fancy crowns?

And what if the missing art pieces were boxes?

Well then.

The boxes would blend right in with the costumes. Who would look twice at Wise Men carrying gold, frankincense, and myrrh? You would expect to see *that*.

Even the Wise Men themselves had been fooled.

For a while.

But, as Timothy had said, the boxes were just too beautiful to be props.

And after they'd heard Bob's story about stolen art, it all fell into place.

The cousins were almost positive that the boxes were Sylvia's stolen artwork and that they themselves had been the perfect hiding place.

But they had to check it out to see if they were right.

Checking things out. It was all part of the detective work. They would take the boxes to their grandmother and ask if they were Sylvia's. Then they would know for sure.

"I still can't believe that odd woman," muttered Sarah-Jane. "First she pretended to

Sylvia that she was Mr. Fitzgerald's assistant so she could steal the boxes. Then she pretended to us that she was some kind of prop lady so she could hide the boxes. On us! She hid them on us!"

"But at least the boxes are safe," said Timothy.

"Don't be so sure," murmured Titus. "She's watching us."

11

Stuffed Animals

The cousins knew better than to make any sudden moves.

Very, very casually they ambled over to a booth filled with homemade stuffed animals. They wanted it to seem as if they were picking out a present for Timothy's baby sister, Priscilla.

"Ooo, here's a cute bunny rabbit, Tim," said Sarah-Jane in a perfectly normal voice, in case the woman came close enough to hear them.

Under her breath she said to the boys, "What are we going to do? If we run, she'll know we're on to her. Then she's sure to come after the boxes."

"But the baby hippo is more unusual," said Titus, making conversation.

Then he murmured, "We just have to act

casual and get home as soon as we can, I guess.
The problem is these costumes. We're sitting
ducks in them. She can spot us anywhere in the
crowd."

"I think I'll come back later and get the
piglet," said Timothy. "Priscilla is crazy about
pigs."

Titus and Sarah-Jane didn't know if he was
making that up. But they realized it didn't
really matter.

Timothy whispered, "We could maybe
ditch the costumes in that alleyway over there.
We can always come back for them later. But

that still doesn't solve the problem. She knows what we look like. And if she sees us without the robes and still carrying the boxes, she'll know something's up."

Suddenly Timothy grabbed his cousins and said urgently, though still whispering, "You guys! Look! Look over there! Do you see what I see?"

Titus and Sarah-Jane scanned the crowds to see what had caught Timothy's attention like that.

They saw the three Kevins, dawdling on their way to dress rehearsal.

The Kevins were wearing choir robes.

12

Decoys

*T*he woman's back was safely turned. The cousins scooted across, grabbed the Kevins, and hauled them into the alley.

"OK, here's the deal," said Timothy quickly before the Kevins could get over their surprise. "We're in big trouble, and we need your help. See that woman over there? The one looking around? Just peek out. Don't let her see you!"

"What about her?" asked Kevin O'Connell.

"She's an art thief, and she's after us," said Timothy.

The Kevins looked at them with interest. "Cool," they said.

So far, so good.

Timothy rushed on. "She's actually after these boxes. It's a long story. But we have to get the boxes back to the artist. Only that woman—the thief—keeps following us. So we need you to change robes with us. We need you to throw her off track so that we can get the boxes away."

"Like a decoy, you mean," said Kevin Jones.

"Exactly!" said Titus. "Will you do it?"

The cousins held their breath.

The Kevins looked at one another and shrugged. "Sure. Why not?" they said.

Timothy could hardly believe his ears. Who would have thought the Kevins would be so helpful?

Quickly, the Kevins and the cousins changed robes.

"OK," said Timothy. "All you have to do is walk around and get her to follow you. But don't let her get a good look at you."

Then Sarah-Jane thought of something important. "But always make it look like you're carrying something. Otherwise, she'll get suspicious. Maybe you could hold your hands together in front of you with the sleeves covering them."

"OK," said Kevin Weston. "Except—maybe we should *really* be carrying something.

That way, we won't forget and accidentally put our hands down."

"Good thinking," said Titus. And Timothy agreed. The Kevins were really getting into this.

They all scouted around the alley and found three good-sized rocks about the same size as the boxes. If the Kevins stayed far enough away from the woman and let their sleeves cover their hands, the plan might just work.

"Is that it?" asked Kevin O'Connell.

"That's it," said Timothy. "We don't think she's in any hurry. In fact, we think she might be waiting until the crowds thin out a little be-

fore she comes to get the boxes back and make her getaway. It's a long story."

But the Kevins looked so interested that Timothy quickly filled them in on how they came to have the boxes in the first place. He finished by saying, "So, if she comes up to you to get the boxes, just play dumb."

The Kevins looked at one another and grinned. "We can handle that," they said.

When the woman wasn't looking, the Kevins slipped out of the alley and wandered away among the booths. They kept their backs to the woman. Then—sure enough—the woman spotted them and followed at a safe distance.

The cousins made themselves count to ten to let the Kevins lead the thief farther away.

Then Timothy, Titus, and Sarah-Jane hid the beautiful boxes in the sleeves of their choir robes.

They slipped out of the alley.

And walked quickly away in the opposite direction.

13

Back on the Horse

*T*he cousins hid themselves in a group of choir kids on their way to rehearsal.

"Hey!" said one of the choir kids. "What are you guys doing here? Aren't you supposed to be the Three Wise Men?"

"It's a long story," said Timothy. He said this in a way that meant he wasn't going to tell it. He had already explained everything to the Kevins. And he knew he was soon going to have to explain everything to his grandmother. So he didn't feel like explaining it all another time in between.

At the house, the cousins found their grandmother in the kitchen, talking to a young woman. They guessed she was Sylvia.

Both ladies looked pretty discouraged.

The cousins' grandparents had fairly strict rules about not interrupting. But Timothy figured this was an emergency.

"Excuse us, Grandma," he said. "But we have two questions. Number one: Is this Sylvia?"

Grandma and the lady looked at them in surprise and said that it was.

"OK," said Timothy. "Question number two is for Sylvia: Do these boxes belong to you?"

Grandma and Sylvia jumped up with exclamations of astonishment and joy.

It took a while—quite a while—to explain how it was that Timothy, Titus, and Sarah-Jane came to have the boxes. And how it came to be that they weren't in costume.

"Well, now, young lady," Grandma said to Sylvia, sounding friendly and firm all at the same time. "I think it's time you got back on the horse."

The cousins knew there wasn't really any horse. It was just an expression. A way of speaking. They knew that if you fell off a horse, you were supposed to get right back on. Otherwise, if you waited, you might get too scared to go riding again.

That was the way it was with any hard thing you had to do. If something bad or discouraging happened, you had to try again right away. Otherwise, if you waited, you might get too scared to try again.

"What do you mean?" Sylvia asked Grandma. Of course, Sylvia probably knew there wasn't really any horse, either.

"I mean," said Grandma, "that you're going to go right back to Mr. Fitzgerald's gallery and show him these lovely boxes."

"Oh, no—I don't know, Mrs. Gordon . . ." Sylvia began.

Timothy thought of something important, so he figured it was all right to interrupt again.

"Look at it this way," he said to Sylvia. "Somebody liked your boxes enough to steal them."

Everyone laughed. And Timothy had to admit that it had come out sounding funny.

"No, I mean it, Sylvia," he said earnestly, one artist to another. "That woman took one look at your work, and she knew it was really good. What she did was really bad. But what she did should tell you your work is good. And

51

if you at least show it to Mr. Fitzgerald, that would be good."

Sylvia stood up straight and picked up her boxes. "OK, I'll do it! On one condition—that all of you come with me."

They stopped on the way to explain to the choir director why the Kevins weren't at rehearsal yet.

The cousins didn't want the Kevins to get in trouble. Of course, the Kevins were almost always in trouble. But it didn't seem fair for them to be in trouble for doing something good.

"Speaking of the Kevins," said Titus. "I wonder if that phony-assistant-prop-lady-thief has spotted the switch yet?"

"I wouldn't be surprised," said Timothy. "She must have come back for the boxes by now."

Sarah-Jane said, "And once she saw that *we* were gone, and the *boxes* were gone . . ."

Timothy and Titus knew what Sarah-Jane meant. And they had to agree. The boxes were safe. But the *thief* was probably long gone.

That's where they hadn't counted on the Kevins.

14

Help! Police!

*T*he cousins and Grandma and Sylvia walked back to the center of town to visit Mr. Fitzgerald's gallery.

They had expected to run into the Christmas-in-July crowds, of course.

But they suddenly realized that something strange was happening.

Rather than wandering here and there, the crowds were gathering in a big circle.

The cousins spotted Bob and John and hurried over to them.

"What's going on?" they asked.

"Beats me," said John. "I just got here. I heard all the commotion and came to see what was going on."

Commotion was right.

From the center of the circle came the sound of shouting.

It sounded like—

It sounded like—

For a split second the cousins just stared at one another.

The Kevins?!?!

Without another word, they rushed through a gap in the crowd, with Grandma and Sylvia following close behind.

No wonder people were staring!

At the center of the circle stood a furious-looking woman—the thief—with the Three Wise Men running in circles around her, yelling, "Help! Police! Help! Police!" at the top of their lungs.

At that very moment, a couple of police officers cleared a way through the crowd to see what all the ruckus was about.

And then Sylvia—who hardly ever spoke above a whisper—stormed into the circle, yelling, "That's her! That's her! She's the one who stole my boxes!"

And the Kevins kept running around yell-

ing, "Help! Police! Help! Police!" until the po-
licemen made them stop.

Everyone said it was the best art festival the
town had ever had.

15

Heroes

*I*t turned out that the phony-assistant-prop-lady-thief was already wanted by the police for a string of art thefts.

So the cousins and the Kevins were Big Heroes that day.

The police made them go over the whole story from the beginning.

And this time, Timothy didn't mind telling it.

In the meantime, Grandma told anyone and everyone that three of these wonderful children were her grandchildren and that the other three wonderful children were well-known boys who went to her church.

"I always wondered what that would be like," Kevin O'Connell said to Timothy.

"What what would be like?" asked Timothy.

"You should know," said Kevin. "What it would be like to have people saying how smart you are. How brave you are. How *good* you are. I always wondered what it would feel like to be really, really good."

"So how does it feel?" asked Timothy.

Kevin grinned. "Good."

It also turned out that Mr. Fitzgerald *loved* Sylvia's boxes.

But people were so interested in them because they had been stolen by a notorious art thief that the boxes were bought up before they could even reach the gallery.

Mr. Fitzgerald asked Sylvia to bring him some more of her work.

Grandma told Sylvia it was high time she thought of herself as an artist and met some other artists in town. The cousins got Sylvia started on that by introducing her to Bob and John.

And finally, it turned out that the Christmas concert was a wonderful success.

Apparently the screaming Wise Men had been great publicity.

"Come to my workshop," Sylvia told the cousins and the Kevins after the concert. "I have something for each of you."

What Sylvia had for them were tiny hand-made Nativity sets from the collection of her artwork.

The Nativity sets were like Sylvia's boxes. All made from everyday objects with great care. All beautiful and good.

"Wise Men for the Wise Men," Sylvia said. "To thank you for all you've done."

Timothy looked at his tiny Magi, bringing their rich gifts to an even tinier Baby Jesus.

It was amazing when you stopped to think about it, Timothy thought to himself. Wisdom and Goodness showed up in the most unexpected places.

Who would have expected the Kevins to come through like that?

Who would have expected Sylvia could make such beautiful art out of ordinary junk?

Who would have expected to find a King in a stable?

The Wise Men certainly deserved to be called wise, Timothy decided. They found an ordinary-looking child in a humble little place.

But the Wise Men never wondered if they'd made a mistake. They knew Goodness when they saw it. So they bowed down before Jesus and gave Him their treasures.

"Thank you, Sylvia!" said Timothy.

And so did all the others.

But just as they were leaving, Timothy thought of something else he wanted to say. He told the others he would catch up to them. Then he went running back to Sylvia.

"Sylvia, can I come watch how you work sometime? Because . . . I like art. And . . . well, you're an artist."

"Sure," said Sylvia. "I'd like that very much. And as for being an artist—I have a feeling you're one, too."

The End

Series for Young Readers*
From Bethany House Publishers

THE ADVENTURES OF CALLIE ANN
by Shannon Mason Leppard

Readers will giggle their way through the true-to-life escapades of Callie Ann Davies and her many North Carolina friends.

ASTROKIDS™
by Robert Elmer

Space scooters? Floating robots? Jupiter ice cream? Blast into the future for out-of-this-world, zero-gravity fun with the AstroKids on space station *CLEO-7*.

BACKPACK MYSTERIES
by Mary Carpenter Reid

This excitement-filled mystery series follows the mishaps and adventures of Steff and Paulie Larson as they strive to help often-eccentric relatives crack their toughest cases.

THE CUL-DE-SAC KIDS
by Beverly Lewis

Each story in this lighthearted series features the hilarious antics and predicaments of nine endearing boys and girls who live on Blossom Hill Lane.

JANETTE OKE'S ANIMAL FRIENDS
by Janette Oke

Endearing creatures from the farm, forest, and zoo discover their place in God's world through various struggles, mishaps, and adventures.

THREE COUSINS DETECTIVE CLUB®
by Elspeth Campbell Murphy

Famous detective cousins Timothy, Titus, and Sarah-Jane learn compelling Scripture-based truths while finding—and solving—intriguing mysteries.

*(ages 7–10)